Get Rich Mitch!

MARJORIE WEINMAN SHARMAT was born in Portland, Maine. She has written over eighty children's books, including the enormously popular *Nate the Great* and the Maggie Marmelstein novels. Many of her books have been picked as Children's Choices by the International Reading Association, and fourteen were Junior Literary Guild selections. Marjorie Sharmat now lives in Tucson, Arizona, with her husband, Mitchell, and the best dog in the world, Fritz Melvin.

Get Rich Mitch!

Marjorie Weinman Sharmat

Illustrated by
LORETTA LUSTIG

AN AVON CAMELOT BOOK

AVON BOOKS
A division of
The Hearst Corporation
1790 Broadway
New York, New York 10019

RL:5.7

The William Morrow edition contains the following Library of
Congress Cataloging in Publication Data:

Sharmat, Marjorie Weinman.
  Get Rich Mitch.

  Summary: After becoming famous for winning a sweepstakes,
eleven-year-old Mitch serves as a model for a bestselling doll and
encounters some of the shortcomings of being a celebrity.
  1. Children's stories, American. [1. Dolls—Fiction.
2. Fame—Fiction] I. Lustig, Loretta, ill. II. Title.
PZ7.S5299Gc 1985 [Fic] 85-8799

First Camelot Printing: October 1986

Printed in the U.S.A.

OPM 10 9 8 7 6 5 4 3 2 1

for Mitch,
who makes my life rich

• 1 •

I know you've heard of me, Rich Mitch. I'm in hiding right now. In the Ritz Royale Plaza in New York City. I'm afraid to show my face. I'm afraid I'll be recognized. Maybe I'll hide out for the rest of my life. I'm only eleven.

When I was plain Mitchell Dartmouth I won $250,000 in the Dazzle-Rama Sweepstakes. So far, so good. After taxes I was down to $135,000. After the set of four personalized swans my mother bought for our front yard was paid for, I was down to $134,702. Then came my father's snazzy wardrobe; my mother's oil paintings of various vegetables; my big sister Lynda's addiction to fifty-dollar haircuts; my expensive present for my best friend, Roseanne Rich; imported parrot food for my pet, Dumb Dennis; and legal fees to Blake Reynolds IV, who charged $120 an hour. I ended up with $68,305.19.

I also ended up being famous. People called me the famous lucky kid, Rich Mitch. That was okay for a while. Until the stampede started. The stampede of people. Who were they after? Me, *lucky* me.

I wasn't thinking about stampedes the day my mother took me to the photography studio. She said she wanted some new photographs of me. I don't like having my picture taken, but my mother said I'd be happy to have the picture to look at twenty years from now when I'm thirty-one years old. My mother also had another reason, a secret

reason that would eventually cause millions of people to be in hot pursuit of Rich Mitch.

"Wear something expensive," my mother said as I got dressed for the photo session. As if I had a choice. My parents had a fancy tailor make me a blazer with gold buttons and wool pants. They bought a silk necktie, a silk shirt, and shoes with gold buckles. Do you know how hard it is to find shoes with gold buckles for boys? They found them. I planned to lose them.

"Don't forget to wear your new shoes," my mother said.

"Shoes? Isn't this going to be a face picture?"

"No, it'll be all of you."

It should have made me suspicious to need new shoes for a picture in a photo studio. My friends have these face and shoulder poses, and that's it. Who needs new shoes? When I'm thirty-one years old, why would I want to see the shoes I wore when I was eleven?

My mother inspected me when I was through dressing. "I don't know if you look sufficiently rich."

"Sufficiently rich?" I said. "I just want to look like me."

"That, too," said my mother. She called to my father. He

came in and looked me over. "Not rich enough," he said. "Isn't that supposed to be a customized haircut?"

"Ormanne's best," said my mother. "Sixty dollars. He raised his prices."

Now my father was actually circling me. "I don't like him from the back," he said. "It's not a wealthy back view."

"I agree," my mom said. "He must look equally rich, front and back."

I was getting confused. Okay, maybe they wanted a picture with my shoes showing. But the back of me? Who goes to a photographer to get a picture taken from the back?

"Look," I said, "is this a show-off picture? What happens if I'm poor when I'm thirty-one and I have this rich-looking picture of myself at eleven? I'll think that I did something wrong, that I became stupid from age eleven on and lost all of my money."

My parents weren't listening. They were both circling me. Then my mother bent down and looked at the top of my head. "The view here could be better."

My father joined her. "Agreed."

I said, "I've got news for you. A photographer is not going to take my picture looking down at the top of my head. You think he's going to bend over like you two and shoot a picture of just the top of my head?"

Mom and Dad answered together. "Yes."

"I don't like to say anything, but the photographer you picked is out of his head. I don't want to go to any nutty photographer." I started to take off my jacket.

"Stop!" ordered my mother. And she started to take off her jacket. My mother has this habit of taking off her clothes when she gets excited. It can get embarrassing in public.

"Please, Mitchell," Dad said. "We didn't pick this photographer. Someone picked him for us. He's tops in his field. You'll be happy you had your picture taken. I promise you will."

"Why?"

"You'll see."

3

Mom and Dad started to fool around with my hair. I gave up and let them. The sooner they fixed me up the way they wanted, the sooner I'd get to the photographer and he'd take his dumb pictures and it would all be over with.

I was wrong. Instead of something being over with, the photo-taking was just the beginning of millions of people trying to get Rich Mitch.

•2•

The photographer was a show-business photographer in New York City. We live in a suburb of the city, and there are several photographers in town. But we went all the way into New York to this guy who had these big, shiny pictures of celebrities on his walls. Did that make me a celebrity? Would the top of my head go up on his wall? My shoes with the gold buckles?

The photographer, Jean-Paul, and his two lady assistants all looked like they were in show business. They were wearing tight clothes, and they had jewelry in their ears. The studio was full of bright lights and white umbrellas and heavy wires snaking all over the place. I figured that this was an expensive deal, but I also figured that my parents weren't paying for the pictures. Jean-Paul said something about a Bucky Glitzer arranging this. Who was Bucky Glitzer? I didn't much care. After I won the sweepstakes I got a free haircut, free clothes, and some other free things. I was used to free.

Mom apologized for the appearance of the top of my head and for my "really terribly average-looking back view."

Jean-Paul circled me while he drank coffee. "Well, at least he doesn't project abject poverty."

"I'm certainly relieved to hear that," said Mom.

Good. That probably meant that she'd be keeping all her clothes on.

"On the other hand," said Jean-Paul, "he's bordering on middle-class."

"What do you mean?" Mom asked as she fiddled with her belt.

Jean-Paul sipped his coffee and stared at me. "It means, essentially, that when one looks at Mitch, one thinks of a modest little house on a small plot of land, clothes bought at an after-Christmas sale, respectable but plain food on the table . . . very, very *middle*, you know."

"We're in trouble?" My mother unfastened her belt.

"But of course not," said Jean-Paul, and he beckoned us to a small room. There were lots of mirrors in the room and a table and chair. There was a bunch of stuff on the table: combs, brushes, and makeup.

Jean-Paul picked up a brush and started to do things to my hair. "You see," he said to Mom, "a little sweep to the side and—*voilà!*—the modest little house on the small plot of land is gone. This is the mansion look."

Mom nodded. "The mansion look," she repeated.

Jean-Paul took a powder puff from a box on the table. He was going to puff me! "No," I said. "That's for girls. I don't wear makeup."

"It won't *look* as if you're wearing makeup," he said, "but it will help to create the illusion we want."

"I don't want an illusion. I want to go home," I said. "I went with my friend Roseanne once when she had her picture taken. She just sat down and the photographer told her to smile and he tilted her head and he aimed and he went click-click a few times and that was that. She got a nice picture, and her parents put it on the piano in the living room for everybody to see."

While I was talking Jean-Paul kept putting makeup on my face. I bet I could sue him for doing that against my will, but I can't find out because my lawyer now charges $150 an hour.

Mom was smiling. "*Now* I see," she added. "The mansion look. Definitely."

I stared into the mirror. My eyelashes seemed very dark

and thick, and my face was pink and smooth. I hoped Mom didn't have any plans for putting my picture on our piano.

One of Jean-Paul's assistants came into the room and said, "We're ready out here. Come this way, Mitch."

I got up and followed her out of the room. "Look what we have for you, Mitch," she said. She pointed to a table that had all my favorite foods on it, including a lot of junk stuff that Mom doesn't let me eat.

Mom had followed me out of the room. She was smiling. "It's for you, Mitch. Eat!"

"I can eat all of this?"

"Every last bit," said Jean-Paul, aiming his camera at me. "Right after we take our pictures. Now think about how this food tastes, Mitch. You *want* this food. Think greed. Think about having the money to buy everything You're rich. You want *everything*. Let me see it "

ing doing," I said.

"Very well," said Jean-Paul. "Just *look* at this food. That's not too much to ask, is it?"

I looked at the food. I *wanted* it.

Suddenly Jean-Paul started to take my picture. "You've got it!" he said. "The expression. Marvelous, marvelous!"

Jean-Paul moved around me like I was a wild animal he was stalking. He took rapid-fire pictures, one after another. He took me sitting down and standing up. For a few shots he made me stand like I was a tin soldier or something, stiff and straight. Then I had to raise and lower my arms and stand with my legs together and apart. Stupid. He took all kinds of pictures of the back of me and looking down at the top of my head.

"I was careful not to cover Mitch's three freckles with makeup," Jean-Paul told Mom as he continued to snap. "Mitch should look human as well as rich."

Jean-Paul must have taken a couple hundred shots of me. Then he said, "Relax," and he pointed to the table full of food. "Want to eat now?"

"Take off your jacket first, Mitchell," my mother warned.

"We can easily replace your shirt, but your blazer is something else again."

"Yes," said Jean-Paul, "that blazer might go to the Smithsonian someday as a genuine artifact of Americana."

I didn't know what he was talking about. I didn't know what this whole dumb picture-taking session was about. I didn't know anything until a week or so later when the lady named Bucky Glitzer came to our house with the pictures.

Then I found out everything.

· 3 ·

We were all sitting around the living room of my house. Me, Mom, Dad, and Lynda, and my wonderful parrot, Dumb Dennis. My parents had just introduced our guest, Bucky Glitzer, to Lynda and me. She was wearing a blue dress, blue shoes, and a blue hat. She was carrying a big blue pocketbook. She either didn't want to be noticed at all or she wanted to be noticed very much. It was hard to tell.

Bucky Glitzer hugged me as if I were a relative or something. "Mitchell Dartmouth in person!" she said.

Lynda kind of sneered. Lynda doesn't mind my being rich, but she's kind of a wise guy about everything that goes with it.

"I know it happened some time ago, but do let me congratulate you on winning $250,000, Mitchell."

"Oh, well, thanks," I said, "but I've only got $68,305.19 left."

Mistake! I'm not supposed to tell strangers about my financial situation. I looked at my parents. They seemed pleased!

Bucky Glitzer sat down. "I'm so glad you brought that up, Mitchell," she said. "I think it's a shame that you can't keep every cent you won and watch it grow. And, Mitchell, that brings me to the purpose of this little visit."

She kept saying "Mitchell" as if she knew me. She crossed a blue leg over another blue leg. Her stockings were blue,

too. She went on. "Mitchell, I work for Tech-Toys, a very large toy company, and you'll be happy to know that we've been observing everything that has happened to you since you won the Dazzle-Rama Sweepstakes."

I wasn't happy to know that.

"We've concluded that you're extremely merchandisable."

"Merchandisable? Is that a word?" asked Lynda.

"No matter. We use it on special occasions in our company when we find something or someone capable of capturing the hearts and minds of the public."

My parents were smiling.

"You, Mitchell, are one of those rare commodities. . . ."

"I'm a commodity?"

"Well, person—in this case, of course. At any rate, you have that rare something that people all over this country will respond to."

"Money?" asked Lynda.

"Yes and no," said Bucky Glitzer. Now she was looking straight at me. "Mitchell, the public thinks you're lucky. You entered a contest and won against overwhelming odds."

"The odds of winning were one in 19,265,000," I said.

"Fantastic. Against odds like that you *won*. Everyone wants to be a winner. But it happened to *you*. You're lucky and you're rich. That's an unbeatable combination."

"Well, maybe," I said, "but there are other things that are important, like—"

"I *know*. Family, right? Good friends, right?"

Bucky Glitzer had all the answers. That made me nervous.

"Mitchell, people want to be like you. They want to identify with you. They want to have a part of you."

"Mitch could sell locks of his hair," said Lynda. "Is that what you're getting at? I want a horse, and if we could sell Mitch's hair or something ... well, it just gets swept up after his haircuts and thrown away."

Lynda was serious. She stops being a wise guy every time she smells a chance to get money to buy a horse. She wants to be a veterinarian someday.

"Good. We're all of one mind and moving closer to our common goal," said Bucky. "But we won't have to sell Mitchell's hair."

"I'm not moving toward any goal," I said. "I don't understand any of this."

"Well, Mitchell, remember when you had your picture taken?"

"I could forget?"

Bucky took a large envelope from her pocketbook. "These are the pictures. We needed a likeness of you from every possible angle."

"Why?"

My mother spoke up. "We were saving the news as a surprise," she said as she took off a shoe and an earring. "And here it is. Mitchell, dear, you're going to be a doll!"

• 4 •

How could they make so many dolls so fast?

Bucky Glitzer's company must have doll-making factories or grandmas on farms or convicts in prisons making dolls nonstop. Must be. All I know is that one day they sprung the doll surprise on me, and it seemed like almost the next day when there were hundreds of dolls ready to be sold.

The doll was called Rich Mitch, and it had a slogan: BE LUCKY! GET RICH MITCH! At first they were going to have the slogan: BE LUCKY! GET RICH MITCH QUICK! But they took a survey and people had trouble saying that one. The doll was dressed in a blazer with gold buttons, a white shirt, a tie, pants, stockings, and shoes with gold buckles. Its hair was parted with a sweep toward the side. But that's not all. The doll came with stuff attached to its wrist: a bankbook, two stock certificates, a deed to a mansion, and an airplane ticket for a trip around the world. They were all phony, of course.

I didn't want to be a doll. It's hard to explain how very much I didn't want to be a doll. A greedy-looking one or any other kind. The Rich Mitch doll looked greedy. It wanted *everything;* you could see it in its face. What if my friends saw it? What if it turned up in a yard sale when I was fifty years old? I could be teased forever. But my parents were thrilled with the idea. Lynda, seeing a horse in her immediate future, was thrilled, too.

"This doll could fail, couldn't it? It could be a big flop?" I asked right after my mother broke the news to me. "It's possible that it could flop before it even got going?"

"I'm afraid that's true of almost any merchandising venture," Bucky had answered. "We're going to produce a limited number of the dolls and test-market them. However, if they're successful, the Dartmouth family could be rich indeed. We're drawing up a contract allowing us to use Mitch's name and likeness in return for handsome royalty payments."

Mom, Dad, and Lynda had gasped at the word *payment*. Then they looked at me as if I controlled the world.

Hoping for failure, rooting for failure, I said okay. I could always pretend that the dolls didn't exist. When I thought about it, and I never had until that moment, there are dolls in stores all over the country, and I hadn't heard of any of them. Dolls are something for babies and little kids. I was safe.

But I wasn't safe. I was shocked by the quick manufacture of the dolls. That was a bad sign. It meant that Bucky's company was right on their toes. They had energy and speed, two qualities I don't associate with failure. They also had plans to include me in their sales pitch. Gone was my plan to ignore the existence of the dolls.

Bucky contacted my parents to arrange for what she called "my first personal appearance with the doll." Since she used the word *first,* I figured she had second and third and fortieth and one hundred and fortieth in mind. She wanted me to show up at our biggest local department store, Garth's, in the doll section of their toy department. She said that a small ad would be placed in our local newspaper.

"How small?" I asked my mother when she told me the news.

"Teeny," my mother answered. "This is just a test to see if shoppers will be attracted to your doll. Bucky warned me that we could be very lonesome standing there in the toy department."

"How lonesome?" I asked hopefully.

14

• 5 •

On Saturday I put on my Rich Mitch outfit—the blazer, the buckled shoes, all that stuff—and Mom and I went to Garth's Department Store. We walked through the store as if we were normal shoppers. Nobody looked at us. We got to the toy department and nobody looked at us. Finally my mother went up to a salesperson and introduced herself as Rich Mitch's mother. This didn't make any impression, so my mother had to explain.

"Oh, yes," the salesperson said finally, in a tired sort of way. She looked at Mom and me as if we were a nuisance. Then she disappeared into a back section and came out with a little sign that read:

BE LUCKY! GET RICH MITCH!
MEET MITCHELL DARTMOUTH,
WINNER OF THE $250,000
DAZZLE-RAMA SWEEPSTAKES, IN PERSON
TODAY, 10 A.M.—NOON.
THEN GET LUCKY LIKE THE REAL MITCH—
GET THE RICH MITCH DOLL.

"Shoppers with poor eyesight are not going to be able to read that sign," Mom said. "The printing is too small."

The salesperson shrugged. "I'm Mrs. Slater. The man-

15

ager of the department is at a meeting. I only work here. I'll go bring out the dolls. They're in back."

"I smell disaster," Mom said, taking off her scarf as Mrs. Slater retreated to the back again.

Mrs. Slater came back with three dolls.

"Three dolls?" my mother gasped. "Where are the others?"

"Others? I'll go look again." Mrs. Slater sighed and disappeared. But she came back dragging a carton full of dolls. "I found these," she said. "We have thirty Rich Mitch dolls. Are you happy with thirty?" Mrs. Slater dumped the dolls on a large table that already had other kinds of dolls on it. The table was overloaded. Some of the Rich Mitch dolls were standing upright, some were falling over, some were between standing and falling.

Mom picked up a doll that was flat on its face.

"Make yourselves comfortable," Mrs. Slater said, and she went back to her counter.

There was no place to make ourselves comfortable. All we could do was stand by the table of dolls and look silly. But Mom was busy standing up dolls. She was worried. "It's almost ten o'clock. Where are all the people? There should be a line forming. That newspaper ad was much too small, too easy to miss." Mom took off an earring.

At ten-twenty Mom and I were still standing by the table, just the two of us, lonesome in a wonderful kind of way. The Rich Mitch doll was a big flop, and Mitchell Dartmouth was going to live happily ever after. I was sorry for Mom, but she'd get over it.

A woman came up and asked Mom where the ladies' room was. I guess she thought my mother worked for the store. It was worse than if nobody came up at all, because Mom had a moment of hope before the woman opened her mouth.

Mom kept arranging the Rich Mitch dolls. She had pushed the other dolls on the table into a heap, after making sure that Mrs. Slater wasn't looking our way. She placed the Rich Mitch dolls in neat rows of threes and smoothed all the papers hanging from their wrists. The dolls were really kind of cute. The only thing wrong with them was that they looked so much like me. They really did. And, of course, we were dressed alike.

Finally someone noticed the connection. A white-haired lady who was carrying four big, empty shopping bags picked up a doll from the table. Then she looked at me. "You're dressed like this doll," she said.

Mom brightened. She pointed to the little sign. "Meet my son, Rich Mitch, and the Rich Mitch doll."

The woman seemed fascinated. "Why, you're the sweepstakes winner and this doll is *you!* What are these papers? A bankbook, two stock certificates . . . incredible. You certainly are a lucky boy. My grandchildren would love these dolls. If I buy a few, will you autograph them?"

Mom answered. "Of course he will."

"Do you take MasterCard?" the woman asked.

"We don't work here," Mom answered. "Mrs. Slater over there will take care of your purchases."

"Good," said the woman. Then she leaned over the doll table, and with her elbow, she started to sweep Rich Mitch dolls into her shopping bag.

"How many grandchildren do you have?" I asked while the woman kept on sweeping.

"Dozens."

Mom clasped her hands together. She was speechless.

"I should have brought a suitcase," the woman said as she dragged her filled shopping bags over to Mrs. Slater. "I'll be back for autographs."

The grandmother had taken every one of the Rich Mitch dolls! Three cheers for her and her dozens of grandchildren. As soon as I autographed her dolls, I could go home!

"There she is!" A man and two women came rushing into the toy department. They were followed by three men and five women. And some kids. Some of the men and women were pointing at the grandmother. The first man kept repeating, "There she is!"

"She beat us to it," a woman said. "She's got all the dolls. It figures."

"What do you mean?" Mom asked.

"That's Maude Cloverdale over there," the woman answered. "She's a doll scalper, the bounty hunter of the doll trade. She buys dolls when they first come out, and then she resells them for a big profit."

"But what if nobody else wants them?" I asked.

"Maude sniffs out the future successes. She has an instinct for dolls. She knows what's going to hit big. And she hits big. Hey, Maude, I'll give you double what you paid."

"Triple," a man said.

More people came. We were getting a crowd. A little girl stuck a notebook in my hand. "Autograph, please. To Samantha."

Mom produced a pen. I signed "Mitchell Dartmouth."

Samantha looked at the autograph. "No. Write Rich Mitch. I want to be lucky and rich like you!" Then she touched me. Her hands were sticky, and I was wearing my expensive blazer. I hoped my mother wouldn't start to take off her clothes.

There is one thing I learned quickly. A crowd produces a bigger crowd. And I learned something else. The Rich Mitch doll appealed to people. They loved it! They said, "Cute!"; "I've never seen anything like it!"; "Adorable!"; "Let's get lucky!"

This was all being said while Maude Cloverdale was holding an auction. "Who will give me two hundred dollars for a Rich Mitch doll?" she shouted as she waved a doll in the air.

Mrs. Slater was tugging at her. "We don't auction in this department."

A man who had bought a doll from Maude was holding it high. "Who will give me two hundred and fifty dollars?"

Samantha was going around yelling, "Get near Mitch. He's lucky. You might catch it."

Suddenly I realized that my mother had disappeared. Then I saw her pushing her way back to me through the crowd. She bent over and whispered in my ear, "I've called the media."

19

"What?"

"This is it, Mitchell. We have a nice, civilized little riot over the dolls. Once the newspapers and TV pick it up, the Dartmouth family will be very very rich. I hope that Mrs. Slater won't spoil everything. She's getting awfully mad."

About fifteen minutes went by. The crowd got bigger. Some of the shoppers on the outer fringes probably had no idea what was going on. But my mother was fuming. "This is a perfect riot, and the media are missing it." Mom took off her other earring and a hair clip.

She didn't have a chance to take off anything else. The crowd started to do it for her. They were grabbing at us and our clothes. "Catch good luck!" a little boy cried as he tugged at my jacket.

"Where are the media at a time like this?" my mother asked as she unglued the boy's fingers from my jacket.

A minute later two women yanked off my jacket and ripped my shirt.

Mom turned to me. "It's time to leave, Mitchell," she said. "Trust your mother's judgment, it's definitely time to leave."

"How?" I asked as someone pulled the gold buckles off my shoes.

"Just push, Mitchell! Push. We can do it."

We pushed. The crowd pushed us back.

The media never came. But the police did. Six officers. I guess Mrs. Slater called them. Or maybe the store's security people did.

They hustled Mom and me into the department manager's office as Maude Cloverdale yelled, "I hear two hundred dollars. Who will give me two hundred and fifty?"

One of the policemen looked interested.

Mom and I collapsed into chairs. My jacket was gone. My shirt was all ripped. One shoe was missing.

"Oh, Mitchell," my mother said, "do you know how difficult it was to find those gold-buckled shoes? You should have kept your eye on them."

The manager got two blankets from the linen department or somewhere, and Mom and I wrapped them around

20

us. We slouched in our chairs, looking woolly and plaid. Someone brought us tea and hot chocolate from the store's restaurant. The policemen stood around while we sipped. Then they hustled us out of the store.

"At least we weren't ignored," Mom said.

· 6 ·

Bucky Glitzer was waiting in a limo outside of Garth's Department Store. She had two photographers with her. They were standing by the limo with their cameras ready. "Get it! Get it all!" Bucky commanded them as the officers escorted Mom and me to a police car. My blanket was dragging on the ground, and one of the policemen tripped over it.

"Super!" Bucky said as she got out of the limo. She went up to one of the policemen. "We'll take Mitch and his mother home."

The policeman looked at Mom and me. We nodded okay.

Mom and I got into Bucky's limo. Bucky waved good-bye to the photographers as we drove off.

"Our clothes!" Mom said. "Look what happened to our clothes!"

"Tech-Toys will gladly replace your clothes," Bucky said. "This worked out perfectly. The mob, in particular, was terrific."

I looked at Bucky suspiciously. I had never heard of a terrific mob. Like, are there good mobs and great mobs and terrific mobs? Bucky was acting as if she were the director. Could she have *hired* some of these people? I didn't see her at the riot. How did she know about it?

Mom didn't have to worry about the media not showing up. She and I and our new blankets were in the newspapers the next day. Pictures of the Rich Mitch doll were in the newspapers the next day. There was even a picture of Maude Cloverdale when she was younger and at the beginning of her doll-scalping career. The newspapers said that Maude had known all about the dolls before she went into Garth's Department Store. The dolls had been her mission. A spokesman for the store announced that Garth's was ordering two thousand Rich Mitch dolls.

"Two thousand dolls!" my mother exclaimed.

"I don't want to be a doll," I said. "I don't want to be a doll two thousand times."

"Cheer up, Mitch," Lynda said. "The Bionic Man has a doll."

"Does it look greedy? Is it wearing gold buckles?"

"Your doll is supposed to bring good luck," my father said. "It says that in the newspaper. And you're supposed to have what's called 'the lucky touch.' "

Some lucky.

• 7 •

People think they can buy good luck. At least the shoppers at Garth's Department Store who rushed to buy the Rich Mitch doll and the good luck that was supposed to go with it thought so. So did the shoppers who lined up all over the country to buy the doll. I couldn't get over it. Sulphur Springs, Texas. Portland, Maine. Miami Beach, Florida. Memphis, Tennessee. Tucson, Arizona. Boston, Massachusetts. New York, New York. Name a city, the Rich Mitch doll was there.

The Tech-Toys Company stepped up production. But the demand for the dolls was bigger than the supply. Stories about people waiting in line for hours to buy a doll started to appear in newspapers. Then came stories about shoppers showing up at four o'clock in the morning to be first in line, and about riots as shoppers fought over the dolls. A California newspaper printed a photo of a lady with "minor injuries" smiling through her bandages as she held up her Rich Mitch doll.

Where did this leave me, Rich Mitch? It left me famous and worried. I was getting kidded at school about the doll. (Except by Roseanne, who said it was an honor to have my own doll.) People on the street were pointing at me. I got pointed at after I won the sweepstakes. But that was nothing compared to this. I was now the object of mass pointing.

One day, around suppertime, my mother sent me to the

24

supermarket to get some hamburger rolls. It was an ordinary walk to the store, the way it used to be before I became Rich Mitch. I guess that most people were inside eating supper.

In the supermarket I got my rolls, and everything was peaceful and pleasant. But, in the checkout line, a woman screamed, "It's Rich Mitch! 'Mr. Good Luck' is standing in this checkout line!"

She grabbed me by the sleeve of my sweater and ripped it. She didn't even notice. She shoved a box of cereal in my face. "Autograph it," she commanded. "Right under the words *bran flakes*."

I was the star of the checkout line. The man in front of me offered me a pen and his bunch of bananas to autograph. This was the first time I had ever autographed a banana. "If the ink leaks through, it might be dangerous," I warned him.

Very fast I went from being the star of the checkout line to being the star of the supermarket. The manager came over and took my picture holding the package of hamburger rolls. He made sure that the store label was showing. He told me that he keeps the camera around to worry shoplifters. He wouldn't let me pay for the rolls.

He spoke to me in this kind of low, conspiratorial voice. "Mitch, if you stick around and sign food for my customers, I'll pay you."

"You'll pay me? I don't get it. Before I became rich, you offered to pay me and my friends to stay away from your store. You said we wrinkled your magazines and made everything sticky."

"I was only kidding, Mitch."

"You didn't even know my name then."

"I do now. Everybody does. So how about it, Rich Mitch? How much will you charge for staying around here and signing? Tell me. You're the boss."

"*Me?*"

"Sure."

That sounded great to me. "I can stay for fifteen minutes," I said. "I have to get back for supper."

I stayed for half an hour. The manager paid me in free magazines. That's the way I wanted it.

I ran home from the supermarket after autographing dozens of cans of fruits, soups, and vegetables; a couple of cartons of frozen yogurt; three packages of TV dinners; a flea-collar box; two jars of peanut butter; one weight and price sticker on a dripping package of chicken parts; and some adhesive stuck around a bunch of broccoli.

I was all excited. It was like Mr. and Mrs. America trusted me with part of their lives, like I was in their kitchens, in their houses, in their families. I must be a very important boy. Fame suddenly felt terrific.

· 8 ·

When I got to my house, I saw a man and a woman at my front door, banging on it. I sneaked around the back and went inside. My mother, father, and Lynda were standing just behind the front door as if they were waiting to catch it if it fell in.

"Who's at the front door?" I asked.

"Fans wanting to see you, I'm sure," my father said. "We're not answering, of course. What happened to your sweater?"

"The same thing that's happening to our front door."

"Flower delivery," called the woman from outside the front door.

"Leave them!" my mother called back.

"They'll wilt!"

"We'll water them after you leave. We'll give them tender, loving care." Mom turned to me. "It's the florist trick. We've also had the phony telegram trick. Someone tried to return a lost dog we don't own and deliver a pizza we didn't order. And, of course, some people wanted their Rich Mitch dolls autographed. You're lucky you're at school and miss most of this."

Lynda piped up. "Sure, Mitch is lucky. That's why he's famous. That doll is going to make us rich. Let them knock down the door. We can afford a new one and a new sweater for Mitch and even a house in a new neighborhood. Keep that banging coming, folks."

My father groaned. "At least we made one smart move. Getting an unlisted telephone number."

"Some smart," said Lynda. "That unlisted number is ruining my social life. Can't I give it out to anybody?"

Mom took off her watch and belt. "No, dear. They'll just sell it to the highest bidder. I'm beginning to get the drift of how fame works."

"Speaking of fame," I said, "I autographed merchandise at the supermarket. That's how my sweater got torn. Boy, was I popular. Bucky didn't hire the people, either. I was famous on my own."

No one heard me over the banging on the door. But the banging made me feel more famous, more important.

It finally stopped. We had a quiet supper and evening. We went to bed early.

At five o'clock in the morning someone peeked into our windows. Campers arrived on our front lawn. Someone pulled up our personalized swans and ran off with them. Mom would have taken off her clothes, but she was mostly undressed, anyway. She loved those swans.

Dad was glued to the window. "About two dozen campers," he said. "They have blankets and transistor radios."

"In addition to dirty clothes and bare feet," Mom said. "I can see their toes under the streetlight."

"They've got pictures of Mitch! For sale!" said Lynda. "And Rich Mitch banners. Somebody's setting up a souvenir stand!"

"Very enterprising," Mom said, forgetting her swans for a moment. "Perhaps I should serve them some coffee and Danish. To start their day off right. Maybe they'd leave if they saw we're good people."

"Forget it. We need police protection," said Lynda.

"I can call my friend, Sergeant Grimes," I said.

Dad looked puzzled. "Isn't he the one who avoids you, Mitch?"

"Well, the last time I called him, he left a message for me that he was on assignment in Pakistan."

"Just great," said Lynda.

My mother sighed. "I loved those personalized swans."

Dad paced around the room. "There's a solution to all of this."

"Let's move to a mansion in a rich neighborhood," said Lynda. "Mansions have thick doors."

My father stopped pacing. "You're almost right, Lynda. But we're not moving."

"Good," I said.

My father turned to me. *"You're* moving, Mitch."

"Me?"

"It's simple. You're the attraction. We simply move *you*."

"Alone?"

Dad put his hand on my shoulder. "No, of course not. Your mother and I will take turns being with you in your hideout until this all blows over."

"Hideout?" Lynda gasped. "That sounds terrible. Will it have cobwebs and rats and stuff?"

"I've been wanting to go to California," I said. "Maybe under a palm tree, by the ocean—"

"No, not that far. Someplace close. New York City. A great place to hide in."

Mom took off a slipper.

Dad went on. "Bucky Glitzer and I had this . . . what you might call an emergency plan. If things got too hectic, which they have."

Mom took off her other slipper. She said, "I didn't go along with it, Mitchell. But now that my swans have been spirited away . . ."

"It's okay," I said. "Bucky Glitzer has some good plans."

Lynda gave me a strange look.

I was getting to like Bucky Glitzer's plans. She's the one who made a doll out of me. She's the one who worked hard to make me famous. Hiring that mob and all.

"Fame has its price," I said. "And I'm willing to pay it. I'll hide out, but I want to take Dumb Dennis with me. We've never been separated."

My father frowned. "I don't know if the Ritz Royale Plaza allows parrots in their suites."

"A suite in the Ritz Royale Plaza!" Lynda screamed. "I'm dying. That's the top of the world!"

"Yes," said my father. "And the Tech-Toys Company will foot the bill."

"Why not?" I said. I figured I was worth it.

• 9 •

Bucky Glitzer showed up the next morning in a blaze of blue. She yelled to the campers on our front lawn, "I'm one of you! I love you!" as she tossed sandwiches and thermos bottles to them.

Dad opened our front door and yanked Bucky inside.

"Beautiful!" she said as my father slammed and locked the door behind her. "Mitch's public. Dirty, disheveled, but the public nevertheless."

Bucky sat down on the living room couch and pulled a bunch of papers out of her blue briefcase.

"Here's the plan for Mitch's escape."

"My escape? Sounds like I'm a criminal."

Bucky fluffed her hair. "Well, darling, celebrities and crooks have much in common. They flee. They keep on the move. They hide. They buy dark glasses and weird wigs and they grow beards if they can. At least you won't be doing *that!*"

"It's okay. Now that I'm famous, I can't expect to live a normal life."

Lynda smirked. "Ho, ho. Listen to the celebrity."

Bucky fluffed her hair again. "Mitch *is* a celebrity. He's famous. Now, having established that fact, we move forward. Literally and figuratively. I call this plan Operation Evacuation."

32

My mother looked at Bucky curiously. "Were you ever in the army? You're so organized."

Bucky didn't seem to hear her. Her head was in Operation Evacuation. She leaned forward. "Time: midnight. Means of departure: limo. Method: elimination of possible pursuers."

"Good strategy," my father said. "We have to be prepared for Mitch to be pursued when he leaves the house."

"I'll say," I said. "It's growing. I'm having trouble now when I walk to school. Roseanne Rich and I used to walk alone. But wait, I just thought of something. I can't leave town because I'll miss school."

"Spring vacation starts this week," Lynda said. "How could you forget *that?* Fame's affecting your IQ."

"Tech-Toys will provide a private tutor for you if you're still hiding out when vacation's over," Bucky said. "Now, getting back to the plan. Tonight at midnight, Mitch, you and your mother will slip out of your house through your basement and escape into a waiting limo."

Dumb Dennis, who hardly ever says anything, squawked.

Bucky got up and hugged Dumb Dennis's cage. "Fabulous parrot. He understands everything, doesn't he?"

"I want to take him with me."

"No parrots allowed in the hotel. Sorry, Mitch. But you can write to him."

"Not funny," Lynda said.

Bucky walked toward the door. "I'll see you tonight."

After Bucky left I looked out the window. Who were the people out there? My friends? My fans? Who?

I went to my room and got my wool plaid blanket. Garth's Department Store had let me keep it. Mom, Dad, and Lynda were in the kitchen. I crept downstairs to the basement, opened the window very quietly, and climbed outside. It would be good practice for tonight. I wrapped the blanket around me, including over my head. I hoped I looked like one of the campers.

I walked up to one of the stands. There were now five.

"Want to buy a Rich Mitch T-shirt?" a woman asked. She was wearing one. It had my picture on it!

"Not right now," I said. "Why are you selling these?"

"I need help with my car loan. If I can sell a thousand of these, I'll own my car free and clear."

"I don't see a thousand customers."

"I have a branch stand. On the corner of Main and Elm. I'm going to open a few branches. I'm going to saturate this town with Rich Mitch T-shirts."

A teenage girl walked up to us. "I'm going to do better than that. I'm going to marry Rich Mitch."

"How do you know that?" I looked at my future wife.

"My horoscope. It says I'm going to marry someone rich and famous."

A man with strange eyes stepped up. "I'm here because I have this vision . . ."

I wrapped my blanket halfway over my face and slunk off. I waited until I was sure no one was looking, and I slipped back into the house through the basement window.

At midnight I was back out the window again. This time with Mom. I had kissed my father and Lynda good-bye. I had told Dumb Dennis that I'd be back soon. Outside, it was quiet and dark. Some of the campers had gone home. Nobody saw us. Mom and I walked through a couple of backyards and then out to the limo that was parked down the street. Bucky was leaning on the limo, waiting for us.

"Good work," she said. "You escaped from the crowd."

"Nobody saw us," I said. "We really didn't escape."

Bucky patted my head. "But of course you did. Mitch, darling, you are famous twenty-four hours of each and every day. Keep that thought. You want to sell dolls, don't you? You want the royalties, don't you? The publicity release from our company will state that Mitchell Dartmouth escaped from thousands of screaming fans and was then whisked away to an undisclosed location."

"Thousands of screaming fans? Where were they?"

Bucky sighed. "Ask yourself, Mitch. Were you really *listening?* Were you really *watching?*"

"Yes."

Mom spoke up. "Perhaps they *wanted* to come, but they had headaches or their cars stalled or their feet hurt . . ."

This conversation was taking place outside the limousine. Inside, a bored-looking driver was staring straight ahead.

Bucky kind of pushed Mom and me into the limo. "Perhaps *hundreds* of screaming fans has a more intimate, personal kind of appeal," she said.

The limousine, with the three of us in the backseat, sped off into the night, headed for New York City.

· 10 ·

By 1:30 A.M. Mom and I were checked into our suite at the Ritz Royale Plaza. Bucky had gone home. Mom and I were alone in our luxury. The suite was fantastic. Thick carpeting, heavy drapes, chandeliers, fresh flowers, everything. We had two bedrooms, a room that was like a living room, two bathrooms, and a kitchen. The refrigerator was full of good things. Four suitcases of clothes were waiting for us, two for Mom, two for me. We had packed them earlier as part of Bucky's plan, and they had been spirited out of our house in big cartons by "delivery men" who were actually employees of Tech-Toys.

Mom stretched out on a bed. "Beautiful," she said. "Tech-Toys is taking very good care of us."

"It's great," I said.

My mother sat up. "Now we have to try hard to keep up our end of it, Mitchell. Let's not forget who you are."

"I know who I am. Mitchell Dartmouth. Rich Mitch. I accept that."

My mother frowned. "No, Mitchell, that's not who you are."

"No? Who am I?"

"William Noyes. And I'm your mom, Mrs. Noyes."

"Since when?"

"Since Bucky checked us into this hotel. Those are our names while we're here. That's who the hotel thinks we are."

"Will the world think that Mitchell Dartmouth has disappeared?"

"No, they'll know that you're just hiding out. Bucky's arranging some interviews and appearances for you. You can't very well show up for them if you've disappeared."

Mom stood up and walked to the window. She opened the drapes. "Look at this view. The New York skyline."

I went over and stood beside her. The city was glittering. It seemed to be my city. I owned it. So what if I had to enjoy it as William Noyes?

The next morning we ordered breakfast from room service.

"Our refrigerator is for snacks," Mom explained. "Room service is for meals."

"Can't we go downstairs and eat in the dining room? Or out to a restaurant?"

My mother shook her head back and forth. "Mitchell . . . William . . . you might be seen."

"You mean, we can't leave this suite?"

"Oh, certainly we can. When you make your appearances on TV. But you must never disclose where you're staying. You wouldn't want to be mobbed here, would you?"

"Nobody's going to mob me in this hotel. It's a stuck-up hotel. It's not, you know, physical. Can't you tell?"

"Well . . ."

"There are probably people here who are much more famous than I am."

I hoped that wasn't true.

"How about my just going to the lobby and buying some newspapers? To see if I'm in them?"

"We can have them sent up, William."

"If I stay in this suite all the time, I might go crazy and forget I'm William."

My mother handed me a fistful of change.

"Be very careful, William."

I unlocked the door and stepped out into the hall. I walked to the elevator and pressed the "down" button. The elevator came. I stepped inside.

"Hold it!" someone shouted.

I don't know how to hold elevators. I don't live in an elevator world. I think you have to press a certain button. I looked for the button while a girl stepped into the elevator. "Thanks," she said.

"I didn't do anything."

"You were trying to. I could tell."

The elevator started to go down. The girl smiled at me. She seemed to be about fifteen or sixteen. She was pretty and skinny, and she had big eyes and straight hair that looked like fancy New York hair. Something expensive had been done to it.

She was staring at me, too. "Who are you?" she asked.

"Uh, some people call me William."

She laughed. "William, huh? Some people call me Wanda Opaque 'cause that's my name. Opaque's a made-up name, but I'm not the one who made it up. I was born with it. Do you have a strange last name, too? Is that why you're not telling me what it is?"

"Some people call me Noyes."

"William Noyes. Are you just staying here for a while, or did you move in permanently? I'm here forever."

"You *live* in this hotel?"

"Night and day. You're in the Falmouth Suite, aren't you? I saw it being cleaned yesterday."

The elevator stopped, and we walked out into the lobby. It was a great lobby.

Wanda walked as if she owned the lobby. "I'm on my way to school," she said. "My chauffeur is bringing the car around."

"A chauffeur takes you to school? Don't the other kids resent it?"

"No. It's a private school. We're all rich except a few kids on scholarships."

"So you live in this hotel, a chauffeur takes you to school, and this is your life? How long has this been going on?"

"Ever since my mother and father split. Mom and I moved here. She said it simplified her life."

40

"What did it do to yours? I mean, do you have friends and stuff?"

"Some from school. But practically nobody from the hotel. Unless you count the doormen, the desk clerks, the bellhops, and the other hotel workers. But most of them come and go."

"Doesn't it cost a pile of money to live here?"

I hoped she wasn't getting tired of my questions. But, to live in a hotel all the time!

Wanda shrugged. "I suppose. I hardly ever think about money. I've been rich all my life, so I don't pay much attention to money."

Wanda waved to a man in uniform. "My chauffeur. See you around. I'm in the Fessenden Suite. Knock on my door. Cheers!"

She ran off. I wanted to ask her how she liked being totally, permanently, all-through-her-life rich.

I felt like leaving the hotel with Wanda. I didn't want to go back to my suite, my prison. But I had to. Mitchell Dartmouth was now a trapped famous person.

I bought some newspapers and went back to the Falmouth Suite, the best-looking jail in the entire city of New York.

• 11 •

Bucky showed up with the news that *Celebrity Chat,* a big TV talk show, wanted to interview me. "They more than *want* you, Mitch," she said. "They're *dying* for you."

"Sounds serious," I said.

My escape to what was called "an undisclosed location" had made me more famous overnight. The story was in newspapers and on TV news shows. Mom thought this was a good chance for her to go on television and make a plea for the return of her personalized swans. But Bucky said it was bad for my image. "The Dartmouth family doesn't plead for anything," she said.

I knew that *Celebrity Chat* was big stuff. I once saw a king on it. He didn't have a country to be king of anymore, but still, a king is a king. I wondered if they made his majesty get his face and hair fixed up. They made me. It was another session like the one with Jean-Paul. I was brushed, fluffed, patted, and smeared. The works. I was wearing my Rich Mitch outfit, of course. By now I owned six identical Rich Mitch outfits. If I got a rip, lost a button, sat on a piece of chewing gum, or had any other kind of clothing crisis, there was always a replacement to put on.

Someone led me to a purple velvet bench with silvery arms and legs. This was the guest bench. I knew it from watching the program. Two men with beards were sitting on either end of the bench. I sat down between them.

I looked out at the audience. Bucky and Mom were sitting in the front row, smiling at me. I hardly had time to smile back before the host of the show, Fritz Melvin, appeared. Suddenly there was theme music, cameras moved in from different angles, and we were on television.

Fritz was holding his mike as if it were an old friend. "Folks," he said, "America is experiencing a phenomenon. People are standing in lines, often in freezing cold and rain, begging, swapping, and alas, sometimes kicking and slugging it out, doing anything to obtain the most coveted product in the country, the Rich Mitch doll. The manufacturer can't make the dolls fast enough. There's an unsubstantiated rumor that someone in Texas purchased a Rich Mitch doll for $12,000. BE LUCKY! GET RICH MITCH! has become our national slogan. Is this merely a craze, or is it a reflection of something deeper buried in our psyches? This is a question tantalizing all Americans even as they dig deeper into their pockets to buy more and more Rich Mitch dolls."

I could tell that the cameras were on me. Would I look stupid if I smiled? What should I do with my mouth? Fritz Melvin knew what to do with his. He went right on talking.

"Today I'm pleased to have as one of my guests, sitting right here on the celebrity bench, Dr. Rheinhold Turkett, professor, psychologist, consultant to industry, and one of our most frequently quoted authorities on the national pulse. And from the world of letters, we have another noted authority, Boone Van Doken, author of the best-seller, *The Age of Mitch: Hope for America*. My third guest needs no introduction. We are honored to have with us none other than Mitchell Dartmouth, known to his legions of fans as Rich Mitch. I think it would not be an exaggeration to call Mitchell Dartmouth the most famous boy in America. Eleven years old, a typical all-American boy who has struck a chord in the hearts and minds of all of us, winner of the $250,000 Dazzle-Rama Sweepstakes, and model and inspiration for the Rich Mitch doll. And ... wait, wait ...

speaking of the Rich Mitch doll, I have a fourth guest. The doll itself!"

Everyone started applauding for the doll. Not for the professor, not for the author, not for me, but for the doll! Fritz Melvin placed the doll on the bench between Dr. Turkett and me. I couldn't stand it. I was jealous of the doll. It seemed to have its own life.

Fritz Melvin sat down on the celebrity bench. He put the doll in his lap. He faced Dr. Turkett. "Okay, Dr. Turkett, what is it? What exactly is happening here? Explain how a doll can take over America."

I was glad that Dr. Turkett got the first question, because I felt too nervous to talk. I was thinking about how many people were watching the show. Bucky had warned me not to worry about that. "They all love you, Mitchell," she had said. "Each and every one of the millions and millions and millions of viewers out there."

Dr. Turkett was relaxed. He stroked his beard. "Well, Fritz," he said, "historically, as our economy fluctuates, we see manifestations of the need for something tangible to hold on to, to embrace, so to speak. In our economy in this particular point in time, the need is particularly urgent. What better to embrace than a doll, a cute, cuddly doll."

Cute! Cuddly! On national TV. Me. He might have been talking about the doll, but it was the same as talking about me. I could never go back to school again. I would live out my life as William Noyes in the Falmouth Suite of the Ritz Royale Plaza Hotel.

Fritz Melvin wrinkled his forehead. "With all due respect, Doctor, I find the Rich Mitch doll rather polished and elegant."

"Exactly," said Dr. Turkett. "When I said cute and cuddly, I was making reference to the Turnip Head doll."

Fritz Melvin smiled. "You're full of surprises, Doctor."

"Actually this was my first one." Dr. Turkett seemed to be smiling back through his nose. He kept talking. "The Turnip Head doll, with its rustic, floppy charm, was gaining a toehold of affection in the hearts of the public. Then

along came Rich Mitch, a doll that's clearly a manifestation of our collective national greed."

"But—" I said.

"Just one moment, sir!" Boone Van Doken's voice boomed. He spoke straight to the audience. *"I'm* rich and darn proud of it!"

Applause.

Boone Van Doken grinned. "Good, good. I'm tired of *rich* being a dirty word. The Rich Mitch doll has made rich respectable. It's given us hope as a country. Did you know that the president has given the doll to his grandchildren? *The Age of Mitch* is what America is all about! Right, Mitch?"

"But—"

"You see? This fine young man is with me all the way. Now, all of you out there who are proud—and I mean *proud*—to be rich, wave your arms."

I folded my arms and waited for the program to be over.

· 12 ·

Wanda Opaque knocked on my door a minute after Mom and I got back to the hotel. I recognized her voice. "Open up," she called. "I know who you are."

Mom called back, "I don't know who you are."

"It's Wanda Opaque," I said. "I told you about her. She lives in a suite on this floor with her mother. It's okay to let her in. She's richer than us. That means she won't tug at our clothes or ask me to autograph her shoes or something."

I opened the door before Mom could object.

Wanda walked in. "I just saw you on *Celebrity Chat* as Rich Mitch Dartmouth. You told me you were William Noyes. How many names do you have, anyway?"

"Only two. And William Noyes is just my hotel name so people won't bother me."

Mom looked nervous. "Mitchell, William . . ." she began.

Wanda extended her hand to Mom. "It's nice to meet you, Mrs. Noyes and Mrs. Dartmouth. And I won't bug Mitchell William. While I was growing up we had so many celebrities wandering in and out of our houses that I hardly knew what an ordinary person was like. You see, I'm chronically rich. It's a kind of disease."

Mom was staring at Wanda. She didn't know what to make of her. "You're diseased?"

Mom had been trying desperately for some time to get what Wanda was now calling a disease.

"You live in a hotel suite all the time?" Mom asked. "Don't you miss your house?"

"Houses," Wanda said. "We had five. Mom sold them all. Now this hotel is home. But, sure, I'd rather live in a house."

"Well, you should tell your mother that," Mom said. "Make her buy back at least one house. Possibly two."

Wanda shrugged. "I've tried. But she doesn't listen. So now I'm just waiting until I'm eighteen in a couple of years. I'll inherit a million dollars or some such figure, and I'll buy my own house."

"A million dollars?" Mom and I both gasped.

"Somebody in your family must have won a lot of sweepstakes," I said.

"Now, Mitchell," Mom said, "it doesn't have to be sweepstakes. There are oil wells, diamond mines—"

"Ice cream," Wanda interrupted. "My grandfather invented Opaque Ice Cream. It caught on and on and on."

"Ice cream?" Mom said. "What a delightful, absolutely refreshing way to get rich. And all those flavors!"

"Being rich isn't everything," said Wanda. "Sometimes it's nothing." She put her hand on my shoulder. "Listen, Mitchell William, if you think you're really into this rich thing permanently, I'll give you some 'rich lessons.' I'll tell you what to watch out for. I'm old money and you're new money. You haven't been at this as long as I have."

"It feels like I've been at it forever," I said.

Mom was interested. "It's nice of you to offer to tutor Mitchell."

"It's not tutoring," said Wanda. "I'm just a kind of guide."

Mom sighed. "Perhaps if I had met you sooner, I'd have learned how to protect my swans."

"Your swans?"

"Stolen."

"Were they insured? Let me tell you about Lloyd's of London. . . ."

Mom invited Wanda to stay for lunch. Wanda was our first real company at the hotel. Bucky didn't count. She was business. Boy, was she business! Mom, Wanda, and I sat around and talked and ate. The lunch itself was from room service, served by a waiter who spoke only to Wanda and only in French.

But who cares. I finally had a real friend at the hotel. And so did Wanda.

• 13 •

Bucky Glitzer had her own ways of measuring fame. First she told me that two out of every ten Americans knew who I was. Then the number crept up to three out of ten. Then four. But she wasn't satisfied. "We want *everybody* in the country, from coast to coast, from sea to shining sea."

Requests for interviews poured in faster and faster after my appearance on *Celebrity Chat*. Fritz Melvin wanted me back as soon as possible. *"Celebrity Chat* has had an avalanche of mail and buckets of phone calls requesting the return of Rich Mitch," Bucky told us one afternoon as she swept into our hotel suite and sat down on a sofa.

I had never heard of buckets of phone calls. How many calls can you get in a bucket? Only Bucky Glitzer knew. And how could I be a hit when all I had said was "But"? Maybe next time I'd have a chance to say something.

Mom was pleased. "I like that show," she said. "I've never seen such a beautiful bench. Perhaps we could get one like it for our house, Mitchell."

Bucky looked down at some papers she had brought in her briefcase. "You're both free next Tuesday, and I'm free next Tuesday, so I'll set it up."

"Wait a minute," I said. "I can go by myself. I don't need two escorts. I'm used to this by now. I know what to do and what not to do. I'm a veteran celebrity."

"By yourself, Mitchell?" Mom said. "Out of the question. This is a big, dangerous city."

"I can take a taxi."

Bucky shook her head back and forth. "No, no, no. A thousand times no. You, Rich Mitch, cannot do anything as *peasanty* as that. The company limo is your means of transportation, and your mother and I are your official escorts."

"I had more freedom when I really was a peasant," I said. "I'm getting tired of this. It's unreal. Fame is a prison."

Bucky quickly pulled a blue pen out of her blue purse. "A wonderful, wonderful quote, Mitch. Remember it for your next interview. 'Fame is a prison.' "

Bucky wrote it down on a piece of paper and handed the paper to me. "Memorize it word for word."

I made a face. Bucky didn't notice. She started to huddle with my mother to discuss "other upcoming Rich Mitch events."

I wasn't needed. I slipped out and went down the hall to Wanda's suite. She was on spring vacation from school. She was supposed to be in Bermuda with her mother, but her mother was too busy with some charity work in New York. So Wanda had to stay in New York, too. Wanda wanted to go to Bermuda, anyway, but her mother said she couldn't go alone. Wanda's mother left her alone so much that I wondered how her mother would even find out if Wanda flew off to Bermuda.

Wanda really understood when I told her my problem. *I* couldn't even leave the hotel by myself. Forget Bermuda, forget the next block.

"Stick up for your rights or you won't have any," Wanda said as she poured me some milk. "I found that out too late. But you're at a good age. Still, you have to wean older people away from what they're used to. I mean, you just can't cut the cord all at once."

"Go on," I said.

Half an hour later I went back to my suite. Bucky's blue legs were propped up on the coffee table. She and my mother were drinking tea.

"Mitch, you mustn't run out of the suite like that," Bucky said. "Please ask permission before you leave. Now, pay attention. Your mother and I have set up your schedule for the next two weeks. Want to hear it?"

"First you hear this," I said. "I'm going to the *Celebrity Chat* program in a chauffeur-driven limousine with my friend Wanda Opaque. She's sixteen, and she knows everything about the world that's worth knowing."

Bucky unpropped her legs. "Are you referring to Opaque Ice Cream Opaque? Marvelous. Possibly there's an angle there. Ice cream, dolls, a tie-in perhaps. We've been thinking of bringing out some accessories for the Rich Mitch doll—a tiny fleet of cars, an adorable mansion, a yacht that floats in the bathtub."

"Forget the ice cream tie-in," I said. "Wanda's just going along as a friend."

"I don't know . . ." Mom said.

Bucky leapt to her feet. "But of course you do. This idea is from heaven. It's all set. Mitch goes in the Opaque limousine."

Mom looked worried. "How will you get home?"

"Wanda will call for the limo when I'm done."

Bucky stuffed her papers into her briefcase. "Mitch has real merchandising acumen. A flair for daring combinations and possibilities. I so admire that."

"Mitchell has always been an admirable child," Mom said.

I could hardly wait for the next Tuesday. I felt free, on my own. Just Wanda and me, sprung from prison.

• 14 •

Wanda's chauffeur, Nathaniel, told us jokes on the way to the TV studio. I never knew that chauffeurs were allowed to be friendly. He told me that his son owned a Rich Mitch doll. I offered to autograph it.

At the studio Wanda got a seat in the front row. I got dusted and powdered and all that stuff, and then I was led out to the purple-and-silver bench. I wasn't surprised to see a man sitting there. Another guest.

But this man was dressed like he worked on a farm! Jeans, faded plaid shirt, scuffed work shoes, an old straw hat. The Farmer in the Dell! Weird. After Professor Dr. Turkett and Boone Van Doken I expected somebody who looked like an authority on something. Maybe the farmer was an authority on growing asparagus, but what was he doing here?

I sat down on the other end of the bench. I didn't want to get too near this guy in case he had hay attached to him. I had to protect my Rich Mitch outfit.

Fritz Melvin zoomed onto the stage and the program began. It was introduction time, I knew that.

"Folks," he said into his mike, "today's program is a battle of giants."

I looked at the Farmer in the Dell. He looked at me. Where were the giants?

Fritz Melvin went on. "In this country we have become

accustomed to corporate giants doing battle. Automobile manufacturers competing for your car dollar, TV networks vying for viewers, cosmetic companies each trying to beautify our national complexions. And the list goes on and on. But today we have as guests, competitors for a product that is uniquely endearing and warm, something we can clasp and cling to, and yes! even love! A doll."

I saw Wanda in the audience make a funny face. I wished I could have, but I was on camera.

Fritz Melvin didn't notice Wanda. He was too busy with himself. He paused to let the word *doll* sink in, and then he said, "I will introduce my younger guest first. But then again, why introduce him? Recently he made such a hit on this program that he was virtually commanded by his public to return. We *all* know him. America's favorite rich boy, Rich Mitch Dartmouth, inspiration for the Rich Mitch doll!"

Wanda applauded madly. That was loyal of her. The rest of the audience did the same.

Fritz Melvin waited for the applause to quiet down. "Our other guest has not been quite so visible, yet he is the genius behind something that is also a national phenomenon, the Turnip Head doll. A hearty welcome to the president of the Figglevista Toy Company, manufacturer of the Turnip Head doll—Mr. Justin Figgle!"

The man on the other end of the bench stood up and bowed. Then he sat down. I wondered if I was supposed to do that. I wished I had Professor Dr. Turkett and Boone Van Doken back. Now I was up against a genius president farmer—whatever that was.

A beautiful girl dressed in not quite enough clothes suddenly appeared, carrying a Rich Mitch doll and a Turnip Head doll. She placed them on the bench between Mr. Figgle and me. Then she walked off the stage.

Fritz Melvin turned toward Mr. Figgle. "Mr. Figgle, we're all wondering—first, is this your normal attire or is it an attempt to publicize the rather plain and folksy nature of your Turnip Head doll?"

Justin Figgle crossed his legs. His jeans had a split seam.

He started to speak. His voice had a split seam, too, like it was supposed to be crackly from calling hogs or something. "I usually work in jeans and an old shirt. I like to think that old, comfortable clothes exemplify the honesty and simplicity of the Turnip Head doll."

"Well, then, are you concerned that this honesty and simplicity have come under attack by the fantastic success of the Rich Mitch doll? Perhaps this is not the year to sell honesty and simplicity?"

The genius president farmer didn't like the questions. "Sir, I'm not selling honesty and simplicity. The Turnip Head dolls are merely reflecting these virtues."

I spoke up. "Mr. Figgle, your company is charging $14.95 for the reflection."

The audience roared. Fritz Melvin beamed. I knew he wasn't interested in being a host. He wanted to be a referee. He hoped his guests would fight.

I'm really not a fighter. And I'm not a wise guy, either.

55

Being a celebrity was making me do things I didn't want to do. Still, Justin Figgle wasn't being very honest about honesty. It was hard not to speak up.

Fritz Melvin said, "Our young friend has made a point here about the commercial aspects of these dolls. They *are* for sale, right?"

Justin Figgle nodded. So did I.

Fritz Melvin walked over to Mr. Figgle and stared hard at him. "In a recent issue of *Making Money* magazine, there was a report that sales of the Turnip Head doll have fallen off thirty-six percent since the introduction of Rich Mitch into the doll market. Could you comment on that, Mr. Figgle?"

"Temporary. Very temporary."

"You have specific plans to stop this downward plunge?"

"I do."

"Could you share those plans with our audience?"

"No."

"Could you give us a . . . hint?" Fritz Melvin smiled broadly.

"No."

Justin Figgle had turned into a dead end. Fritz Melvin was left with me. He turned in my direction. "Are there any plans to increase sales of Rich Mitch?"

I was stuck. I wished Bucky was here. I knew there were plans, but I didn't know if I was supposed to tell. I took a chance. "Well, the Rich Mitch doll already comes with stuff attached to its wrist. A bankbook, two stock certificates, a deed to a mansion, and an airplane ticket for a trip around the world. And now . . ."

"None of this is real. Right, Mitch? We can't hope to use the ticket, for example, to fly to Paris?"

"You could hope," I said. "But that's about it. Okay, this is all paper stuff. Our new plan is to manufacture some accessories. A mansion, cars, a yacht . . . all in miniature, of course."

Justin Figgle looked interested. What if he copied the

56

idea? But what kind of accessories could a Turnip Head doll have? Its own miniature vegetable garden? Tiny Weeds?

I tried to sneak a look at the Turnip Head doll on the bench. It had a soft face with a sweet smile. Its limp body was dressed in faded clothes. You could easily hug this doll. I liked it.

Fritz Melvin was in trouble with the program. Justin Figgle was a strange man. He had clammed up. How long could I talk about a yacht you can float in the bathtub?

Not long. Fritz Melvin tried a new angle. "What are you going to do when the Rich Mitch phenomenon fizzles?"

"It won't fizzle," I said. I knew Bucky would want me to say *that*. "But I'm getting lonesome for my ordinary life. I miss it. Like, I'd like to go into a supermarket and not be asked to autograph packages of food. Know what I mean? It's great to be asked, but it's not something a person would want to do forever. And I have this friend Roseanne who's my real friend no matter what, but I don't know if the new people I meet are my real friends because they just think of me as Rich Mitch."

Suddenly I remembered Wanda sitting out there. I looked straight at her. I said, "But I did meet this real friend, Wanda. Well, she thought I was William . . ."

William! I couldn't talk about William, the other me, hiding out in the Ritz Royale Plaza.

"Go on, Mitch."

"Um . . . *fame is a prison!*"

The audience loved that one. I was rescuing the show! Justin Figgle was giving me dirty looks.

· 15 ·

I was happy when the show was over. I wanted to get back
to the hotel. No, I wanted to go home! I was missing my
father and Lynda and Dumb Dennis. I hoped Lynda was
feeding Dumb Dennis regularly. That was supposed to be
her job while I was away. I was even thinking it would be
nice to have Wanda come with me and stay at my house for
a while. Wanda needed a house again. Mom would be glad
to have her, too. They got along great over that French-
talking lunch we had back in our suite.

People were swarming around me, congratulating me on
the show. Wanda pushed her way toward me through the
crowd. "You were great," she said. "But speaking of prisons, let me know when you're ready to escape from this
one, and I'll call Nathaniel."

"I'm ready," I said.

"One moment!"

It was Justin Figgle. He walked up to me, shaking a few
hands in the crowd along the way. "Would you care to join
me for lunch?" he asked. His voice had changed. It was
smooth and very low. I could hardly hear him. It was as if
he were telling me a secret that he didn't want the crowd to
hear.

"Lunch?" I answered in a low voice, too. I couldn't believe
it. Maybe he liked me after all. I looked at Wanda. She
shrugged as if to say it was up to me.

"This is my friend Wanda," I said. "We came here together, and we're supposed to go home together. In her limousine with her chauffeur."

"I can take you home after lunch, Mitchell," he said.

I noticed that he said "Mitchell." He wasn't inviting Wanda.

"I wouldn't go without Wanda," I said. "We came together. We go home together."

"But her chauffeur can take her home. You just said so."

"No. It's both of us or neither of us."

Mr. Farmer in the Dell wasn't going to get me to dump Wanda. It wasn't such a big deal taking Wanda, so what was the problem? At last he said, "Very well, the both of you. And then you'll be driven home."

"Okay," said Wanda. "I'll call my chauffeur and tell him he doesn't have to pick us up."

"I'll take care of that," said Mr. Figgle. He took out a small pad of paper from his jeans pocket and a pen from his shirt pocket. "Just give me his name and telephone number, and one of my aides will call him."

"Well, thanks," said Wanda. She told Mr. Figgle Nathaniel's name and phone number. Then she said, "Also tell Nathaniel to tell Mitch's mother that we're going to have lunch with you."

Mr. Figgle was busy scribbling away on his pad of paper. Then he tore off the sheet he was writing on and, without turning around, tossed it over his shoulder to a man who was standing behind him. The man caught it. I guessed that he was an assistant to Mr. Figgle and that he stood behind him all the time. That's why Mr. Figgle could aim without looking. The man read the paper and nodded.

Mr. Figgle hustled us to a car that was waiting for him out front. A man was in the driver's seat. Wanda and I got into the backseat. It looked like a very expensive car. Maybe it was bought before sales of the Turnip Head doll went down thirty-six percent.

Mr. Figgle got into the front seat beside the driver, and we drove off.

· 16 ·

"We're going to my house for lunch," Mr. Figgle announced from the front seat. "It's in the suburbs."

"This is nice of you, Mr. Figgle," I said. "I didn't mean to insult your doll or anything on TV."

"Don't worry, I have a plan," Mr. Figgle answered.

Wanda nudged me to keep quiet.

We drove for about an hour. Maybe two. Some suburbs. Maybe Mr. Figgle's house was in another country.

Wanda finally asked, "Where exactly is your house, Mr. Figgle?"

"Out. Way out."

The neighborhoods were getting spectacular. Big old houses set back from the street with lots of trees, hedges, green lawns, columns, fountains. Wanda seemed bored. I guess she was used to this kind of neighborhood. But suddenly she got alert. She started to study each house as we drove by.

"That's one of my five houses!" She yelled and pointed at the same time. *"That* one. With the hand-carved rice gods from Borneo out front. Hey, it's for sale. If it's still on the market in another two years, I'm buying it back. I wonder how many times it's changed owners since I lived in it."

On the next street we pulled up to another house that had a FOR SALE sign in front of it. It looked like a huge

60

antique from the outside. Inside, there was probably lots of heavy furniture, drapes, dust, and gloom.

"Prime antique," Wanda whispered to me. "If this is his house, he'll have a problem unloading it."

"This is my home," Mr. Figgle announced.

I felt bad. Maybe he had to sell it because of the Rich Mitch doll.

"I'm moving to an even better neighborhood," he said, "just as soon as I carry out my plan."

The car stopped. Mr. Figgle jumped out. "Come," he said to Wanda and me. He started to walk up the front path. We got out of the car and followed him. The driver got out of the car and disappeared.

Mr. Figgle opened the front door of his house. I expected to be hit by dust and roving spiders. He flung the door open wide. There was a huge front hall, and beyond it, a living room or something. It was hard to tell what the room was supposed to be. It was covered with *toys!* And so was the front hall. Little toys, big toys, windup toys, puppets, dolls, two train sets snaking around the floor, board games, stuffed animals.

"Look!" Mr. Figgle said as he pulled a toy elephant's tail. A lamp went on.

"Listen!" said Mr. Figgle. He pressed a red button on a toy that looked like a traffic-light game. Music started to play.

"Press *green!*" he said to me.

I hesitated.

"Press!"

I pressed. A whole chorus of children's voices started to sing with the music.

Wanda whispered to me. "Wacko. Ultimate wacko."

Things got more weird when we went into the dining room. Mr. Figgle told us to sit down at the table. Then he excused himself. "I'll be back in a moment. Enjoy the view."

The view was the dining room table. It was covered with a nice tablecloth and pretty dishes and silverware. So far, so good. But in the middle there was a centerpiece. Mom

uses them when we have company for dinner. They're usually flowers or a fruit arrangement or something like that. But this centerpiece was a gold statue of the Turnip Head doll! It must have been three feet high.

"A gold Turnip Head doll!" I said. Gold and turnip heads just didn't seem like a good combination.

Wanda felt the statue. "It's only gold-plated. But it's still wild."

"What's wild?" a deep voice said, interrupting us.

A man carrying trays of food walked into the dining room. He was the same man who had driven the car. I wondered if he was the cook, too. He was a heavy guy who looked like he lifted weights every hour. He was a little scary, even though it's hard to appear scary when you're carrying potato salad and pickles.

Wanda answered the question, sort of. "Everything looks just lovely," she said. I noticed that sometimes Wanda said all the meaningless things grown-ups were expected to say. She was probably brought up that way.

Mr. Figgle reappeared. He was dressed in a three-piece suit, and his hair was slicked back all white and gleaming. His shoes were shiny and black. Wanda started to mutter figures under her breath. She was adding up how much Mr. Figgle's wardrobe might cost.

"What happened to your other clothes?" she asked. "The ones that weren't worth $3,497?"

"Oh, *those*. Those were just image clothes to promote the Turnip Head look."

"You mean the Farmer in the Dell is an act?" I blurted out the question before I had a chance to stop myself.

"Naturally. Look at the clothes *you're* wearing. They're not real, are they, Mitch? You dress up for the public and I dress down."

"The man's got a point," Wanda said with a little sigh.

"My toy company means everything to me," Mr. Figgle said, sitting down beside me. "My family has been in toys for four generations. It all started with a squeeze toy that you could crush in your hand, and then it would uncrush! It

63

was a work of genius. That was followed by the magnetic marble. Brilliant! Watch it seek its target!"

Mr. Figgle got up from the table and then got down on his hands and knees. He took a marble out of his pocket and rolled it across the floor! It disappeared around a corner.

I was glad Wanda was with me. I was glad she was older than me. I needed someone I could trust who could tell me honestly if this man was nuts or just eccentric. But we couldn't talk in front of him.

Mr. Figgle looked up at me. "Want to try it?"

"Not right now."

Mr. Figgle came back to the table. Edmund—that's what Mr. Figgle called him—brought in plenty of food. Salads, hamburgers, fries, and some dishes covered with white sauce and mushrooms. I went for the hamburgers and fries, but Wanda ate the white sauce-and-mushrooms stuff.

The Turnip Head statue on the table seemed to be staring at me, challenging me with its gold-plated eyes.

Wanda said, "Interesting-looking statue you have there, Mr. Figgle."

"Ah, yes! The Turnip Head doll is our masterpiece, the cream, the star of the Figglevista Toy dynasty. The most huggable doll in the universe." Mr. Figgle turned toward me when he said that. Then he said to Wanda, "Did you know we did hug tests before we got this doll perfected? Would you like to hug a Turnip Head doll?"

"After lunch perhaps," Wanda said.

"I'll keep the offer open," said Mr. Figgle. "This doll saved our company. We were headed for bankruptcy. The public got bored with the magnetic marble years ago. Our choo-choo trains caught on for five minutes. I'm talking trouble, young lady. The public simply wasn't tuned into imaginative toys. Until our Turnip Head triumph. It turned our company around, put it back on its feet, made Figglevista a proud name once again."

Wanda was looking at her watch. It had been a long ride out to this place, and it would take a long time to get back to the city. Mr. Figgle seemed to be in no hurry. He could talk Figglevista for hours! Why was he explaining all this stuff to Wanda and me? I was his chief rival. If the Turnip Head doll was the cream of his company, I was the one who was turning it sour. Maybe he'd think that was a funny joke. Maybe he wouldn't.

• 17 •

At last Edmund cleared the dishes away and brought dessert: strawberry cake that he had made with his own hands. I could imagine him crushing the strawberries with his bare fists.

Wanda ate her cake fast. Then she said, "I hate to eat and run, but Mitch and I should be getting back."

"But no!" Mr. Figgle protested. "The fun is just beginning. Edmund will call home for you and say you'll be delayed."

"Well . . ." Wanda looked at me.

I thought about being stuck back in the hotel again. Mr. Figgle was weird, but it was kind of an adventure being here in this house. It was also uncomfortable because of the doll business. I should get back to the hotel. That was my decision. But before I could say anything, Mr. Figgle stuck a piece of paper in my hand. "My dear young man, I don't even have your autograph."

Maybe I should stay awhile longer. I had a real fan here. Lunch. An autograph. I signed: "Best wishes to Mr. Figgle from Rich Mitch Dartmouth."

I always carried a pen with me, now that I was famous.

I handed the paper back to Mr. Figgle. He looked at it. "That's a fine autograph," he said. He handed me another piece of paper. "However, I must admit that I would truly treasure an autograph with the saying you made such a hit with on TV. 'Fame is a prison.' "

"Sure," I said. I wrote, "Fame is a prison. Rich Mitch Dartmouth."

Edmund was looking over my shoulder. "I'd like one of those," he said. "But a little different." He handed me a piece of paper. "Could you write, 'To Edmund Weeks. After I've gone away, I will think about the strawberry cake. It's one of my favorite things. I'll be back for more.' "

"Could you say that slowly?"

Wanda was getting impatient. I wrote fast. I was thinking that maybe we could stay another half an hour or so. These people were so friendly.

"Let's stay another half an hour," I said.

"Okay, Mitch," Wanda said. "But we have to reveal to them where you're living so they can call your mother."

"And they have to call your mother, too," I said.

"My mother's out for the whole day," Wanda answered.

I was sorry I'd mentioned her mother. She never seemed to be home. I wondered if she appreciated Wanda. I hoped that when I moved out of the hotel and back home, Wanda and I would keep on being friends.

"Call the Ritz Royale Plaza and ask for Mrs. Noyes in the Falmouth Suite," I said to Edmund. "Please tell her I'm still with—"

Edmund interrupted me. "I know what to do."

"Well, it's a secret that Mom and I are staying at the hotel, so don't spread it."

"I don't spread secrets," said Edmund, and he left the room with some dirty dishes.

Mr. Figgle rubbed his hands together. "Have either of you ever seen a doll factory?" he asked. "Where dolls are actually manufactured?"

"No," I said.

"It's an experience I've missed," said Wanda. Under her breath I think she said "thankfully."

"Well, how would you two like to see where the Turnip Head doll is made? It's just a hop and a skip from here."

Wanda looked puzzled. "A doll factory is a hop and a skip from here . . . from this neighborhood?"

"Well, perhaps several hops and several skips," said Mr. Figgle.

"I think," Wanda said, "that we should just skip it."

"But it's practically on the way home," said Mr. Figgle.

"In that case, lead on, Mr. Figgle. Okay, Mitch?" Wanda really wanted to go home.

"Okay."

Edmund came back. "Did you reach my mother? What did she say?" I asked him.

"All is well," he answered, and he grabbed some more dirty dishes with his big hands.

"Could you give us a few more details?" asked Wanda.

"No."

Wanda kicked me under the table. Then she kind of gave me the eye.

She had the right idea. It was definitely time to leave this strange place.

· 18 ·

We were back in Mr. Figgle's car with Edmund at the wheel. As we rode along, Wanda seemed to be very interested in the scenery. "I had another house around here somewhere," she said, "but I just don't remember any factories."

"My factory doesn't look like any factory," Mr. Figgle said, turning around from the front seat. "It's kind of cute, as factories go."

Wanda kept looking at the scenery. And her watch.

We reached a highway. Wanda said, "It's already been twenty minutes, Mr. Figgle. I'm afraid that Mitch and I just don't have time to see your factory today. Some other time perhaps. Please tell Edmund to take us straight home."

Wanda said the last sentence in a kind of party-manners voice.

Mr. Figgle was facing front again. He didn't turn around, but I could see one side of his face. It was smiling. "Oh, I can't do that, my dear," he said.

"What do you mean, you can't do that?" Wanda dropped her party-manners voice.

"I just can't take you home right now," Mr. Figgle said. "Not for another three weeks."

"What?" Wanda and I both kind of gasped.

"Don't be alarmed," Mr. Figgle went on, still not turning around. "It's going to be fabulous. We're on our way to a private airport. We're all going to California for three weeks."

California? That was my dream! Ever since I won the sweepstakes, my number-one goal was to go to California.

But not this way.

"Wasn't that a fun lunch we had?" said Mr. Figgle. "It was just a preview to show you what a marvelous time we'll have in California."

"It wasn't a fun lunch," said Wanda, "and I don't understand this."

"You see," explained Mr. Figgle, "the Rich Mitch doll is ruining sales of my beloved Turnip Head. If the trend doesn't stop, Figglevista will be forced into bankruptcy. Now, if the real Mitch is removed from circulation for three weeks, he can't give interviews, he can't go on TV shows, he can't promote his doll. The Rich Mitch doll will fade. I know all about this sort of thing. I watched my magnetic marble die. The Rich Mich doll will become as forgotten as my marble. I know the ups and downs of the toy industry and the public. And this is the plan I worked out."

"You mean the one you mentioned on TV?" I asked.

"Yes. It was only partially formed then. But when you uttered those perfect words, 'Fame is a prison,' my plan solidified. You see, Mitch, the public knows you're jaded and tired of all this fame. You announced it before millions of people. And now, when your note appears, saying that you've gone away for three weeks—"

"Stop!" said Wanda. "What note? Mitch didn't write any note."

"And I never will," I said proudly.

Mr. Figgle finally turned around again. "But you already have. Your note reads: 'Fame is a prison. I wish to think things over. I've gone away. It's for the best. I'll be back in three weeks. Rich Mitch Dartmouth.'"

Mr. Figgle waved a piece of paper. "It's all here. In black-and-white or blue-and-white or whatever color the ink was."

Wanda groaned. "It's dawning on me," she said. "Those

70

autographs you wrote, Mitch. They must have copied your handwriting."

"Exactly," said Mr. Figgle. "My multi-talented Edmund here is also a forger."

Edmund nodded in recognition of this added talent.

"Edmund drives, cooks, waits on tables, and commits forgery. He's also my bodyguard."

Edmund nodded again.

"All the words in this note were in your autographs with the exception of *over, in,* and *three,*" said Mr. Figgle. "Edmund and I couldn't think of a way to work those in. If you would be so obliging as to give us one more autograph, Mitch, using the words *three, in,* and *over* or *over, in,* and *three.* Your choice of order. Perhaps you could work them into a nice saying . . ."

"Get lost," I said.

Mr. Figgle shrugged. "We don't really need them. It was just a thought. To make the note all tidy and perfect."

"I don't suppose you ever called Mitch's mother," Wanda said.

"No. Edmund left the room in order to forge the note, not to make a phone call."

"But what about the message Wanda gave you at the TV station?" I asked. "You wrote it down and tossed it to a man in back of you. Oh, I get it. He was in on the plan. I saw him nod."

"No, I haven't the vaguest idea who that person was," said Mr. Figgle. "He was a perfect stranger. I didn't write down the message Wanda gave me. I wrote: 'Life is just a bowl of cherries. Pass it on.' Then I simply tossed the paper into the air in back of me."

"Look," said Wanda. "This is totally nuts, and I'm going to miss my tennis lessons and ballet lessons."

"Not nuts," Edmund said. "Smart."

"Edmund," I said. "Your last name isn't really Weeks, is it? You just wanted me to write that down for the note, didn't you?"

"Edmund has several different last names," said Mr.

71

Figgle. "He needs several in his various lines of work. By now he must have forgotten the one he was born with."

"Finch," said Edmund. "But we didn't need that for the note."

Everything was getting clear. Now I knew why Mr. Figgle didn't want to invite Wanda for lunch. He was only out to get *me!*

"I'll go to California with you," I said, "if you send Wanda home."

"Oh, no . . ." Wanda began.

Mr. Figgle sighed. "I'm truly sorry if Wanda has paid for those ballet and tennis lessons in advance, but she has to come along now. If we let her go, she'd give away our plan."

"But after three weeks everybody will know, anyway," I said, "and you'll go to jail. You'd better stop right now while you can."

"My dear Mitch, I'm too rich and powerful to go to jail. And if that weren't enough, my lawyers are too rich and powerful to *allow* such a thing."

Wanda nodded. "He's probably right."

"But this is kidnapping . . ."

"I don't use indelicate words like that," said Mr. Figgle. "You'll love my place in California. Palm trees, a swimming pool, trillions of toys to play with, and Edmund will be your personal slave, won't you, Edmund?"

"I'll do my best," said Edmund.

Mr. Figgle looked out the window. "And now I'll let the two of you mumble and grumble together in the backseat, hatching little escape plans that won't work. You can't escape from a car going sixty miles an hour on a highway or from a plane for obvious reasons. Oh, Edmund will be our pilot."

"We don't have to mumble and grumble, Mr. Figgle," Wanda said. "The police will be looking for us. We haven't been seen or heard from since the TV show. And Mitch's mother worries about everything. I mean, calling Scotland Yard is within the realm of possibility for a person like her."

I thought about my mother. She must have taken off all her clothes by now! Poor Mom.

"I anticipated that," said Mr. Figgle. "But don't forget, *I* know how fame works. Mitch's mother probably thinks he's still being swamped with admirers at the TV station."

I reclothed my mother.

• 19 •

Mr. Figgle kept on talking. "There's a radio station a few miles from here. Edmund is going to leave off your note there in an envelope marked 'From Rich Mitch Dartmouth.' You wrote those words for us, you know. At any rate, I'm sure the envelope will be opened immediately, and I predict that within an hour everyone will know that Mitch is safe."

Wanda wasn't licked. "And you think it won't look suspicious for this, this . . . hulk—excuse me, Edmund—to leave off a note from Rich Mitch?"

Mr. Figgle chuckled. "Not when he shrugs and says, 'Some kid all dressed up in a fancy blazer handed me five bucks to leave this here.' Then, of course, Edmund will simply walk out."

I began to believe that Wanda and I would be mumbling and grumbling together in the backseat.

But then I had an idea. "Mr. Figgle, I think my disappearance will make me and my doll *more* famous."

"Oh, absolutely," said Mr. Figgle. "For about five minutes. Then the public will accept your not being around and it will all turn to ho-hum. I intend to vigorously promote Turnip Head while you're out of sight. Edmund has already lined up several California interviews for me and my Turnip Head."

Wanda touched my arm. "We're in trouble," she whispered. "He's brilliant and he's weird, and it's a rotten combination and we've got to get out of here."

"Any ideas?" I whispered.

Wanda put her mouth to my ear. "When Edmund stops at the radio station . . ."

I put my mouth to Wanda's ear. "Yeah, that's what I've been thinking."

Wanda and I kept rotating mouths and ears as we whispered together.

"I bet he knows we're thinking of it," she said.

"We have to try."

"Okay. After Edmund gets out of the car and goes into the station, we'll bolt out of the car and run."

My ear was tickling from Wanda's whispering, but it wasn't the right time to complain. I asked, "Where will we run to? What direction?"

"Let's separate. This will give us two different chances. All we need is one. I'll run down the street and go into an alley or something . . . whatever's around. But you, you're famous. You can start yelling on the street or dash into the radio station. Yell, *'Help! I'm Rich Mitch and Mr. Figgle is trying to kidnap me!'* Anything like that will do fine. If you get caught and I escape, expect to be rescued very soon. It isn't like you're being kidnapped by an anonymous stranger. Mr. Figgle is a public figure."

We leaned back and were silent. And tense. I could hardly wait to pull up in front of the radio station and try our plan. On the other hand, I felt like waiting forever.

• 20 •

"We're here," Mr. Figgle said as the car slowed down in front of the radio station and stopped. Wanda and I got ready to make our move. But we tried to act natural. "Good-looking building," I said.

Wanda and I watched Edmund. We didn't want to move too fast or too slowly. We had to wait until he got out of the car, and then, just as soon as he walked into the radio station, we would bolt. I would go first because I was sitting on the side next to the curb. Wanda would follow immediately. We wanted to leave at the same instant, but that would have meant that Wanda would be getting out on the traffic side of the car. We were smart enough and calm enough to decide against *that*. Maybe we were smarter than Mr. Figgle.

We weren't.

Mr. Figgle suddenly opened the window on his side of the car, yelled, "Hey, madam," tossed something at a lady who was about to enter the radio station, and said, *"Go, Edmund!"*

Our car sped off. I looked through the back window. The lady had turned and picked up whatever Mr. Figgle had thrown.

"Change of plans," Mr. Figgle said with a chuckle.

"No, that was your original plan," I said. "You made up the other one about Edmund going into the station."

76

Mr. Figgle kept chuckling. "Clever young man. The two of you were just waiting for your chance to escape, and this was supposed to be it, I imagine."

"Don't be so smug, Figgle," Wanda said. She had dropped the "mister." She was furious. "You just goofed. You like to toss, don't you? You tossed something to a man after the TV show, and now you've tossed that forged note to a lady on the street. She'll probably just read it and think it's a joke and throw it away."

"No. She was on her way into the radio station," Mr. Figgle said. "I'm sure she'll hand it to someone in charge."

"Well, maybe she will and maybe she won't," said Wanda.

"Oh, she will," said Mr. Figgle. "One more thing. I wrapped the little package in a one-hundred-dollar bill. It's a rich gesture and goes nicely with Mitch's note. Sort of a theme . . . like he's throwing away his riches."

"Wonderful," said Wanda in a defeated voice.

I spoke up. "Maybe she noticed you and us and the car."

"No. All she got was a quick look, if that. And this is an expensive car. Rich Mitch leaves in style. It fits the theme."

Wanda groaned.

Mr. Figgle turned and looked at us. "I do wish that you both would enjoy this a bit. I've gone to a great deal of trouble, you know."

"We believe it," said Wanda.

I whispered to Wanda, "We have to think of something else."

It's hard to think of something when you're in a moving car. But I tried.

When we stopped for a red light, I tried to roll down the window and shout "Help!" But the window was fixed so it wouldn't open. Wanda tried to hand-signal to a car that was stopped next to us. But the people in it just smiled and waved.

Mr. Figgle seemed invincible.

It was getting dark. Wanda and I didn't bother to whisper anymore. There was nothing to whisper about.

"I have to go to the ladies' room."

It was Wanda, speaking up in a firm voice.

"We don't have one in the car," Mr. Figgle answered.

That almost surprised me. Mr. Figgle seemed to have thought of everything else. He turned to Edmund. "Look for an isolated gas station or something along that line."

I wondered if this was part of an escape plan of Wanda's. I couldn't whisper and ask her. It would seem like we were conspiring again.

Edmund, who was good at everything else, was good at finding a deserted-looking gas station. It was on a lonely road, it was dumpy-looking, and it had a front like it might be closed or open . . . sort of a nothing, nowhere look. Edmund parked just beyond it.

"This looks fine," Mr. Figgle said. "Now we're all getting out together and walking to the rest room. Just a group of weary travelers. Fortunately it's almost dark."

We got out of the car. That's when I found out that Mr. Figgle had control of the door openings. Wanda and I couldn't have bolted in front of the radio station, anyway.

I looked around anxiously. If I could only get near enough

to someone to shout, "Help! I'm Rich Mitch and I'm being kidnapped."

There was no one.

I wished I knew if Wanda had a plan.

We found the rest room. Wanda went inside while Mr. Figgle, Edmund, and I waited outside. It seemed like we were waiting a long time. I remembered all the escape-from-rest-room movies and TV shows I had seen. A person goes in the door and out the window. Boy, I was tired of watching that old trick. It was too simple and obvious and wouldn't really work in real life.

Mr. Figgle sighed. "She's taking a long time, and I know why. She's busy writing messages on the wall. So dull. We'll just go in and wipe them off when she's finished."

That was it! Poor Wanda. In there, writing her heart out.

Mr. Figgle sighed again. "Whatever is she writing in there? A book? A brief message would have sufficed. Doesn't the school system teach you children to express your thoughts in simple, concise language?"

At last Edmund knocked on the door. "We're waiting," he said.

Wanda didn't answer.

Mr. Figgle spoke up. "Would you kindly communicate, young lady? Are you all right?"

No answer.

I was getting worried. What if Wanda had fainted or something?

"Kindly respond," said Mr. Figgle. "If you don't, we're going to force open the door."

No answer.

Edmund fiddled around with the lock. He knew locks. It didn't take him long to open the door.

The rest room was empty! And there was an open window!

· 21 ·

I learned something. No matter how clever a person is, no matter how much he plans ahead and analyzes and anticipates, he can get tripped up by something plain and simple. Wanda had remembered the old restroom trick and used it. And now she had disappeared into the darkness.

"Hooray!" I shouted. "You've had it, Mr. Figgle. Wanda's on her way to report you."

"Not so fast," he said. "Edmund, drive around. We'll catch her."

They hustled me back to the car. Edmund drove up and down the narrow road. I was looking to see if there were any stores or places open where Wanda could get help. Still, would she risk trying to get to them and being spotted by Edmund and Mr. Figgle? I didn't see anything except trees. Maybe Wanda was hiding out there, waiting for us to drive off. It would probably be futile for Edmund and Mr. Figgle to try to find her in the dark.

I hoped Wanda wouldn't try to hitch a ride in a passing car. There weren't very many. But that seemed to be what Mr. Figgle was hoping for as we drove back and forth on the road. At last he said, "Stop, Edmund. Strategy time. We have to change our basic strategy."

To what? I wondered.

"Obviously we can't take the chance of going to the airport now," Mr. Figgle said. "So I think we'll spend the night at one of our abandoned doll factories. And tomorrow we'll start out fresh with a brand-new plan."

A *brand-new* plan? When Wanda escaped, I thought I was practically free myself. But what if I wasn't? I was happy for Wanda. But I missed her.

Now there was just me alone.

• 22 •

We were on our way to Mr. Figgle's factory. I was taking stock of my situation. *I* knew what trouble Mitchell Dartmouth was in, but what did the outside world know at this minute? Had the forged note been released to the public? Was my disappearance a major news item? What about my family? Were people looking for me?

And Wanda. Did she manage to get to the authorities? Or was she hiding, shivering in the dark woods somewhere?

Now I was really outnumbered. Just me against Mr. Figgle and Edmund. They were more alert than ever. They weren't going to be fooled again. I was getting tired. Maybe I could fall asleep and wake up free—if I slept for three weeks.

I slept for three hours. Or two. Or however long it took to get to Mr. Figgle's factory. It was a big old building surrounded by a vacant lot. It looked abandoned. As we got out of the car Mr. Figgle became a host again. "You have your choice of accommodations, Mitch," he said. "But I recommend the dollhouse."

"The *dollhouse?*"

"Yes. It's a little house out back complete with living room, kitchen, bedroom, and bath. It's a bit smaller than a human's house but quite comfortable."

And escapable? I didn't ask that question. But I was thinking it.

Mr. Figgle said, "It's completely surrounded by a quite attractive fence *eight feet high.*"

He knew what I had been thinking.

"Let's go around the back and you can have a look," he said.

Mr. Figgle walked in front of me. Edmund walked behind me. There seemed to be nothing to see in back. It looked like a vacant lot. Open. No fence.

"I feel like sleeping under the stars," I said.

"You can if you wish. But *inside* the fence." Mr. Figgle pointed. "There."

In a far corner of the lot was a very cute fence, if you go for fences. It had vines and stuff growing on it. Mr. Figgle walked over to it and stood in front of its gate. Then he unlocked the gate by beeping some kind of gadget he had in his pocket. "Come," he said.

Edmund and I followed him. Inside the fence, and completely enclosed by it, was a little house that looked like a gingerbread house from a fairy tale. The roof looked like it was made of frosting.

We had to bend to get inside. There were dolls and toys everywhere, and tiny furniture. The bed in the bedroom was a little shorter than me. My feet would probably hang over it.

"Everything in this house works," Mr. Figgle said quite proudly. "Figglevista built it for a toy convention. It was a sensation. After the convention, we set it up here. Well, what do you think?"

"I'm sure that every doll in the world would love to live here," I said, "but I want to go home."

"Three weeks," said Mr. Figgle. "Now, as you've no doubt observed, the fence is much taller than you. And if you think the vines on it will help you scale it, forget it. They're made of silk and they'll simply rip if you grab onto them. Also, the fence is slippery as an eel. I tell you these things in advance because I want to save you a great deal of wasted effort. Have I forgotten anything?"

"Yes. What's my other choice for accommodations?"

"Inside the factory with Edmund and me. Sleeping on old doll stuffing. It scratches and it makes me sneeze."

"Pleasant dreams," said Edmund.

They left, making sure that they locked the gate behind them.

I sat down on the living room couch. I felt like a giant. Maybe I could huff and puff and blow this house down. But I'd still be inside that fence.

I went outside and examined the fence and the locked gate in it. They looked like they were made of wood. But they felt hard like steel. And slippery as an eel. I looked up at the top of the fence. I didn't feel like a giant anymore. I felt like a dwarf.

I went back inside and walked around the house. Here I was. Rich. Famous. A prisoner. A prisoner in a dollhouse!

I went into the bedroom and stretched out on the bed. My feet had no place to go, and neither did my head, the bed was so small. A small bed! Small furniture! I could carry or push the furniture to the fence, pile one piece on top of another, and climb up and over to freedom!

I gave the bed a big push. But it didn't push. It just stayed still. It wouldn't move. It was attached to the floor! So was all the other furniture in the house. I tried everything, including kicking.

I tripped over some toys. I remembered the toys in the main house, the ones where you could press buttons and music would start and lights would turn on and who knows what else. I thought about Mr. Figgle and the way his mind worked and didn't work. I started to fool around with the toys, pressing whatever buttons I could find. I got a symphony orchestra to play, a window to open, and a doll to dance. Big deal. But I kept pressing buttons. Since one of them had opened a window, maybe one could unlock the gate.

I pressed every button I could find. No luck.

Three weeks isn't forever.

I got ready for bed. There was real toothpaste in the tiny tube in the tiny bathroom. The plumbing worked, too. The

84

soap dish was full of tiny, round pieces of soap, all in pink and green except one that was silver. Silver soap? I picked it up. It wasn't soap. It was a marble. I rolled it on the floor. It rolled out of the bathroom and turned a corner. It was one of Mr. Figgle's magnetic marbles. It disappeared.

I started to look for it. I don't know exactly why. It must have taken me fifteen minutes, but I found it in the bedroom attached to the bed frame. It was magnetic, all right, and I wondered what else. I wondered just what was inside it, what made it do whatever it did.

I pulled the marble away from the bed frame. I kept staring at it. Then, clutching it in my hand, I walked outside and touched the marble to the lock on the gate. The gate swung open!

I ran like crazy.

And ran.

Two blocks from the factory I saw a house with its lights on. I banged on the front door shouting, "Help! Help!" I forgot about saying I was Rich Mitch. I probably didn't have the rich look anymore after all I'd been through.

I saw some drapes open.

Sometimes it's better to be a kid than a grown-up. I don't know if the people in that house would have let an unknown grown-up in. But they opened their front door for me.

It was all over.

· 23 ·

Right now I'm more famous than I've ever been. I am famous all over the world. Possibly ten out of ten people now know who I am. After I got kidnapped, GET RICH MITCH! was no longer just a doll slogan. It became an international battle cry. Everyone started to look for me. And for Wanda, too. Here's what happened.

The lady in front of the radio station delivered the forged note and contributed the one hundred dollars to start a GET RICH MITCH! reward fund. The news of my disappearance quickly went from the radio station to the media all over the world. Mom went on TV and announced that "my son Mitchell would *never* run away from home. Also, he would never misspell the word *three*." Mom held up the forged note for all the TV viewers to see. "*Three* spelled *t-h-e-r-e-e*," she said. "Impossible!" When Mom started to remove her belt, the TV cameras moved to an interview with a psychic who claimed she knew exactly where I was—in an ice cream parlor in Las Vegas, Nevada.

Wanda and I had a lot of laughs over the misspelled note. Edmund, who was supposed to be able to do everything, couldn't spell. And Mr. Figgle hadn't bothered to check up on Edmund's work.

Wanda told me, and the rest of the world, what she did after she escaped through the rest-room window. She made her way through what seemed like "a million miles of woods" until she reached an all-night restaurant and bar. Their TV set was on, and there I was on the screen telling about my escape from the dollhouse. Wanda hugged everyone in the restaurant, bought them all scrambled eggs and toast, and then telephoned Nathaniel to chauffeur her home from her kidnapping.

Wanda bought me and my family a present because she said that I helped to change her life. Maybe I did. Her mother was so happy to have Wanda back safely that she dropped all her activities and took Wanda to Europe for the three days that were left of Wanda's spring vacation. But even better than that, they're buying a house. It probably will be the one that Wanda used to live in—the one with the FOR SALE sign in front of it. But Wanda isn't sure. She took a liking to Mr. Figgle's house, so she might buy that one instead. Mr. Figgle won't be using it for quite some time. His lawyers weren't rich and powerful enough. Mr. Figgle is in jail. Along with Edmund.

But he's probably happy. His plan succeeded, in a way. He saved the Figglevista Toy Company from bankruptcy. As a criminal he became as famous as me. In jail he immediately began to arrange for the production of a Farmer Figgle doll that looks just like him in his Farmer in the Dell outfit. Faded plaid shirt, jeans with a split seam, scuffed work shoes, an old straw hat.

The Farmer Figgle doll and the Rich Mitch doll are now in direct competition, and the Farmer in the Dell is winning.

Bucky is furious. She's just walked into our hotel suite. She slams her blue briefcase down on the coffee table. "Figglevista!" she says. "Between the Turnip Head doll and the Farmer Figgle doll, they've cornered the rustic market!"

My mother doesn't understand this. "But, Bucky, we've got the rich market. Isn't that better?"

Bucky shakes her head back and forth. "Not this week, not this month. Maybe not ever again. Rich is out of style."

"Does this mean I can go home?" I'm looking at Bucky and trying not to smile. Her unhappiness is my happiness, but I can't do anything about that.

"Sure. Go," she says. She pats my head. "Try not to take it too hard when your life returns to normal, Mitch. When you're ignored, when you're a nonentity."

"I'll try."

I'm going to be a real person again! I'm going to have a normal life! I'm going home!

I'm packing. But I'm not going home right away. Wanda's present to me and my family was four airplane tickets to California. California at last!

First-class, of course.